I0784165

Spirits of St. Augustine
A Haunted Coloring Book of Rhyming Tales

Written by: L.R. Corbett
Illustrated by: L.R. Corbett
Edited by: Carla M. Dean, U Can Mark My Word
ISBN: 979-8-9879553-8-3

DISCLAIMER:

The stories and illustrations in this book are based on local legends and the author's creative interpretation of St. Augustine's ghostly lore. While inspired by real locations and reported sightings, the depictions of spirits, buildings, and events are products of artistic imagination and may not exactly represent historical records or eyewitness accounts. This work is intended as an entertaining exploration of St. Augustine's rich paranormal heritage rather than a definitive historical document.

All characters appearing in this work are fictitious or artistically rendered. Any resemblance to real persons, living or dead, is purely coincidental.

The author/illustrator has taken creative liberties to enhance the storytelling and visual appeal of the book. Readers are encouraged to explore St. Augustine's official historical resources for factual information about the city and its landmarks.

Spirits of St. Augustine
A Haunted Coloring Book of Rhyming Tales

Step into the shadowy streets of America's oldest city with "Spirits of St. Augustine," a unique coloring book that brings local legends to life through eerie illustrations and captivating rhymes.

Explore the city's most haunted locations as you color, from the ancient Castillo de San Marcos to the towering lighthouse, where restless spirits still roam. Each page features a different ghost story told in verse, based on real sightings and local lore that has been passed down through generations.

Meet the spectral residents of St. Augustine:
- The mischievous lighthouse girls
- The forlorn Miss Mabel, forever waiting for her lost love
- The grumpy Miss Fay, still guarding her dilapidated home
- And many more ethereal inhabitants!

As you bring these illustrations to life with your own artistic touch, you'll uncover the rich history and enduring mysteries that make St. Augustine a paranormal hotspot.

Perfect for:
- Teens and adults who love ghost stories
- History buffs fascinated by America's oldest city
- Art enthusiasts looking for a unique coloring experience
- Anyone seeking a spine-tingling journey through St. Augustine's haunted past

WARNING: Some content may be too intense for younger children. Recommended for ages 13 and up.

Grab your colored pencils and prepare for a ghostly adventure that will spark your imagination and send shivers down your spine!

This Book Belongs To:

SUMMONS

Welcome to St. Augustine, a historic place of mystery.
The oldest city in the USA, it holds tales of ancient history.
With its cobblestone streets and centuries-old walls,
It hides secrets and spirits inside the shadowy halls.

Where Spanish explorers once did roam,
Ghostly residents now make it their home.
So, turn the page if you dare to peek
At the haunted tales of which we speak.

The Lighthouse Spirits

Our tale begins at the lighthouse shore,
Where waves crash and seagulls soar.
Four little girls who played nearby
Used a cart for rollercoaster rides.

The cart tipped over one fateful day,
Into the ocean, swept away.
Three young lives were lost to the sea.
One girl survived the tragedy.

The others--Eliza, Mary, and Ellie--
Still play at the lighthouse, or so they tell me.
Dressed in old clothes from a time long past,
Their spirits remain, their joy unsurpassed.

Sometimes you'll hear laughter on the stairs
Or see a small figure sitting there.
With a book in her hands, she seems so real.
But blink, and she'll vanish. Oh, what a ghostly deal!

Watch your shoelaces as you climb the tower.
They might get tied together by an unseen power.
The girls love to play and have some fun,
Hiding and seeking until the day is done.

So, keep your eyes open as you explore.
You might spot the girls from days of yore.
They'll be in this old lighthouse by the sea.
Their spirits still playing, wild and free.

The Spirit of Osceola

At Castillo de San Marcos, strong and tall,
A brave warrior's spirit roams the wall.
Osceola, the Seminole leader so bold,
Was imprisoned here in days of old

He fought for his people with all his might,
But was captured by trickery, not in a fair fight.
In the fort he stayed, within a cell so small,
His spirit unbroken by the sturdy wall.

Though his body failed, his legend grew.
And now his ghost appears in view.
Some say they've seen him on moonlit nights,
Standing guard high up on the fort's heights.

His long hair flows; his eyes gleam bright,
A reminder of his people's plight.
He watches over the old coquina fort,
Where his freedom was unfairly cut short.

So, when you visit this ancient place,
Look up at the walls, and you might see his face.
Osceola's spirit, forever free,
Guarding the fort by the shimmering sea.

The Echoes of the Old Jail

Painted pink to fool the eye,
The Old Jail's walls reach to the sky.
Don't let its color lead you astray.
For within, the worst did stay.

Both men and women, wicked and mean,
Endured conditions rarely seen.
Cramped and dark, with little care,
Their anger and pain still linger there.

Now the empty cells aren't quiet, they say,
For ghostly sounds come out to play.
The clank of chains rings through the night,
And phantom footsteps cause a fright.

Visitors sometimes catch a whiff
Of odors making noses sniff.
While barking dogs no one can see
Add to the spooky mystery.

Listen close, and you might just hear
Wails of sorrow or shrills of fear.
And if you feel a touch so cold,
It might just be a prisoner's soul.

So, as you tour this jail's domain,
Remember those who lived in pain.
Their spirits linger, some believe.
In the Old Jail, they'll never leave.

The Ximenez-Fatio House: Whispers of the Past

On Aviles Street, America's oldest way,
Stands a house with tales of yesterday.
Built long ago, its coquina walls
Hold secrets in its rooms and halls.

Miss Fatio's house, a place to stay,
Saw all sorts of folks each day.
Merchants and soldiers, weary and worn,
Found a bed from night till morn.

Thirteen souls, they say, did pass
Within these walls where shadows cast.
Their spirits linger, some believe,
In rooms and hallways, reluctant to leave.

When twilight falls on autumn nights,
The house reveals its spookier sights.
Many locals dare to tell
Of guests whose stays did not end well.

So, visit this haunted house if you dare,
For spine-chilling frights to share.
In St. Augustine's historic scene,
It's where spirits of the past still convene.

XIMENEZ-FATIO HOUSE

The Oldest Wooden Schoolhouse

On St. George Street, you will see
A wooden schoolhouse filled with mystery.
The oldest one that's still around,
It's where history and spirits abound.

Kids once learned their lessons here.
Now it holds secrets from yesteryear.
Strange sounds and sights some say they've seen,
In this schoolhouse where souls convene.

When tourists leave and the day is done,
Some say the mysteries have just begun.
For in the quiet of the night,
Strange things occur just out of sight.

A lady in white, a gentle ghost,
Is seen at night more often than most.
She peeks upstairs with curious eyes
Or gazes in mirrors as time goes by.

Sometimes she looks out to the street,
As if someone she hopes to meet.
Is she a teacher from long ago
Or a mother whose love still shows?

The sounds of children fill the air,
Though no one living can be found there.
A sense of watching, ever near,
Makes visitors feel someone's here.

So, if you visit this school so old,
Keep your eyes open and you might behold
A glimpse of history come alive,
Where spirits of the past still thrive.

Flagler College's Ghostly Founder

Where Flagler College stands so grand,
The Ponce de Leon Hotel once did span.
Built by Henry Flagler, a man of wealth,
His spirit, they say, still walks in stealth.

In halls adorned with Tiffany glass,
Students sometimes feel a presence pass.
Could it be Henry checking his creation,
Still proud of its grandeur and elevation?

In the dining room, so opulent and bright,
Some have seen a figure late at night.
A man in an old-fashioned suit and tie,
Watching diners with a keen eye.

Up in the towers, where few dare to go,
Comes the sound of footsteps, quiet and slow.
And in the courtyard, when all is still,
A ghostly laugh might give you a chill.

Young Henry Flagler, they sometimes see,
A boy on the grounds playing happily.
Perhaps reliving his childhood dreams
In this place he built, or so it seems.

So, if you visit this college sometime,
Keep your eyes open and you might just find,
A glimpse of Flagler through time's haze,
Still watching over his grand hotel's days.

The Spanish Military Hospital's Tale

In old St. Augustine, a building stands,
One of Florida's first healing lands.
The Spanish Military Hospital, they say,
Has many stories from a long-gone day.

Doctors worked with what they knew,
To help the sick and those injured, too.
Though methods back then were not the best,
They did their job with earnest zest.

In 1821, there was a surprise.
The repairmen couldn't believe their eyes.
They found bones beneath the hospital floor
Of Timucuan natives from long before.

Now some who visit feel a chill,
Or hear faint sounds against their will.
Are they echoes from the past
Of those whose stories here still last?

This building holds both facts and tales
Of healing arts that did prevail.
A place where history comes alive
And memories of old still survive.

So, if you pass this infirmary,
Remember all its history.
For in these walls, now empty and cold,
St. Augustine's past is boldly told.

The St. Francis Inn's Lily

In St. Francis Inn, a tale unfolds,
Of Lily and her love so bold.
A slave girl fair, in days long past,
Met a soldier, their love to last.

In secret, they'd meet on the third floor,
Their forbidden romance they would explore.
But fate was cruel, their love not free.
The family found out, as you'll see.

They tore them apart despite their plea,
Leaving Lily as sad as she could be.
In the attic room, where love once bloomed,
Lily's heart broke, her spirit doomed.

Now Lily's Room, as it's known today,
Is where her ghost is said to stay.
She moves small things with gentle care,
A presence felt upon the stairs.

From behind, some see her form,
A fleeting glimpse and then she's gone.
Her soldier, too, in a red coat bright,
Sometimes appears in the night.

Locals claim this tale is true.
In his red coat, they see him, too.
While Lily is shy, not showing her face,
She still haunts this old St. Augustine place.

So, if you stay at St. Francis Inn,
Be kind to spirits that dwell within.
For Lily and her soldier dear,
Still seek their love, year after year.

Tolomato Cemetery: Whispers of History

In the heart of old St. Augustine,
Tolomato Cemetery can be seen.
The oldest planned graveyard in our land,
Where history and mystery go hand in hand

Once a burial ground for the Guale tribe,
Now a thousand souls here reside.
From bishops to slaves and all between,
Each stone tells a tale if you're keen.

Ancient oaks with Spanish moss sway,
Guarding secrets of yesterday.
Convicts, clergy, and children, too,
All rest here beneath skies of blue.

A small white chapel stands at the back.
Of stories and legends, there's no lack.
But remember, young friends, as you pass by,
To show respect for those who lie.

In Tolomato's peaceful embrace,
St. Augustine's past has found its place.
A testament to times long gone,
Where memories and spirits still live on.

The Casablanca Inn's Watchful Widow

On the bayfront, the Casablanca Inn
Holds stories of where smugglers have been.
Its white walls gleam in St. Augustine's light,
But during Prohibition, it hid secrets at night.

A clever widow, who ran this place,
Found a way to keep it with grace.
When times were tough and the law was strict,
She helped rum runners with a trick.

The innkeeper, they say, would wave a light,
To signal rum runners in the night.
From her window, a lantern's glow
Told ships when it was safe to go.

Now, years later when night falls dark,
Some say they see a ghostly spark.
A light that flickers in the gloom,
From the widow's old boarding room.

Her restless spirit keeps her post,
Over the inn and the bay's wide coast.
Perhaps she waits for ships long gone
Or guards her secret until dawn.

Guests sometimes hear soft footsteps pace
Or feel a chill in the empty space.
The scent of perfume wafts through the air,
Though no one living passes there.

If you visit this inn by the shore,
Keep your eyes open because there might be more.
A ghostly lantern's flickering glow
Could be the widow's signal, swinging low.

The Tale of Miss Mabel at Casa de la Paz

Casa de la Paz, a grand old inn,
Welcomed Miss Mabel, her honeymoon to begin.
With her new husband, she arrived in town
To explore St. Augustine of such renown.

They strolled the streets, so quaint and old,
Enjoying their time as their love unfolds.
But one clear day, her husband said,
"I'll go fishing," and off he sped.

A storm came suddenly, wild and strong.
Miss Mabel waited all day long.
She watched the window, wracked with fear,
Praying her love would soon appear.

Though search parties combed sea and shore,
Her husband was seen never more.
Miss Mabel shut herself away,
Her heart grew heavier with each passing day.

Now some say Mabel never left.
Her spirit stays, though she's bereft.
Guests sometimes glimpse a ghostly sight,
A woman with luggage late at night.

She moves small things around the place,
Like crystal tops, without a trace.
"When are we leaving?" guests might hear,
A whispered question, soft and clear.

On stormy nights, when winds howl strong,
Some say they hear a mournful song.
Is it just gusts that moan and weep,
Or is it Mabel's sorrow running deep?

So, if you visit this grand old place,
Be kind to Mabel's lingering grace.
For in Casa de la Paz, they say,
A honeymoon story lives on to this day.

The Tale of Judge Stickney's Teeth

In Huguenot Cemetery, beneath the ground,
Judge Stickney's rest was not quite sound.
Though buried with honor, his peace was brief,
For his story took a turn beyond belief.

His children wished to move him, you see,
To Washington, D.C., where he longed to be.
But as they worked to move him with care,
Grave robbers struck when no one was there.

During a break in the digging process,
Thieves snuck in, causing such a mess.
They stole his teeth, a golden treasure,
Leaving the judge without his pleasure.

These weren't just any teeth, but a special set
Made of gold, a prize to get.
The thieves had struck so quick and sly,
Leaving the family to wonder why.

Now Judge Stickney's spirit, they often say,
Wanders the graveyard night and day.
Perhaps he's searching, with haunted zeal,
For the teeth that someone dared to steal.

R.I.P.
R.I.P.
R.I.P.
R.I.P.

Miss Fay of Cuna Street

On Cuna Street, not long ago,
Lived Miss Fay, a name to know.
Her face always wore a scowl.
Her temper quick, her words so foul.

She made her mark in our town's story,
With a personality far from glory.
Mean to neighbors, mean to all,
Miss Fay's sharp tongue, everyone recalls.

Miss Fay worked at the luncheonette,
A frown on her face and wearing a hair net.
At home, she liked to be alone
In her house that creaked and groaned.

One day, she called a man for repairs
Because she needed to fix her rickety stairs.
But Miss Fay thought she knew best
And sent the worker off, distressed.

In her haste, she rushed downstairs.
She tripped and fell. Oh, what a scare!
Sadly, Miss Fay passed away that day,
But some say her spirit chose to stay.

Now in the house, strange things occur.
Bumps and creaks, lights that blur.
Some say they see an older face,
Peering from the window with little grace.

If you pass by on a moonlit night,
Look to the second floor and you might
See Miss Fay's shadow, stern and cold,
Frowning down, her presence bold.

Her piercing gaze might make you quiver.
Her icy stare will make you shiver.
So, hurry past and don't linger near
Where Miss Fay's spirit brings such fear.

KEEP
OUT

The One-eyed Ghost of Scarlett's

George Colee, a man with one eye,
Built a house in 1879.
For his war service, land he was awarded,
Eighty acres, his efforts rewarded.

He planned to wed, but love went astray.
His bride-to-be chose not to stay.
Though heartbroken, George found once more
Someone to share his life, a new love who he adored.

But fate had plans, both dark and grim.
In his bathtub, death came for him.
How it happened, no one knows.
It's a mystery that only grows.

Was it revenge from love long past?
Or did his new bride act so crass?
Perhaps war's shadows played their part
In stopping George's beating heart.

Now Scarlett's Bar stands where he dwelled.
George's spirit has not been quelled.
A gentle touch, a chilly air,
Remind us that he's still right there.

If you visit, don't be afraid
Of the one-eyed ghost and choices made.
Raise a glass to George's tale,
A mystery that time cannot veil.

LINGER

As our ghostly tour comes to an end,
We hope these tales did not offend.
St. Augustine's spirits, both far and near,
Are part of what makes this city dear.

From lighthouse to fort, from jail to inn,
These spectral stories make history begin.
So, next time you walk down an old cobblestone street,
Remember the souls you just might meet.

For in America's oldest city, they say,
The past and present dance every day.
Thank you for joining our haunted quest
In St. Augustine, where spirits never rest.